This book belongs to:

A CHILDREN'S STORY BOOK

GINGER
THE FOUNDLING

Told and illustrated by Dolly Rudeman

✳

This Series includes the following titles:

GINGER THE FOUNDLING
ROLY-POLY-BEAR
TABBY AND TOMMY
DANNY THE DEER

One warm summer morning Mother Waggle went to the brook to give her children a bath. The little ducklings waggled along in front of her, quacking loudly. Suddenly the first little duck stood stock-still and did not make a sound. Mother Waggle ran quickly to him to see what was the matter. "Oh, what a dear little pussy!" she cried, when she saw what had frightened her little son. "You needn't be afraid of him." The chattering around him wakened up the little pussy who had been curled up sleeping under the forget-me-nots. He looked at Mrs. Waggle and her children with big round eyes. "Who are you, and where have you come from?" asked Mother Waggle. "I am Ginger," said the pussy, who was still just a kitten, but he did not know where he had come from. Mrs. Waggle thought Ginger much too young to be alone in the world and decided to take him under her wing and look after the little pussy.

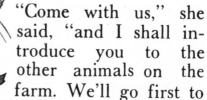

"Come with us," she said, "and I shall introduce you to the other animals on the farm. We'll go first to the Mouse family who live beside the water. My children like to play with the little mice and they always have lots of fun." So Ginger got to know the Mouse family and was soon good friends with them. The little ducklings, the mice and the pussy played together the whole day long while Mother Waggle and Father and Mother Mouse watched that the games did not become too rough, because they had soon seen that Ginger was a real tomboy who liked rough games and was not afraid of anything. The little ones had such fun together that the ducks quite forgot to go swimming, as they had first intended to do. Mrs. Waggle did not mind that for once and she decided to give her children — and Ginger too — an extra good wash the next day. When it was evening and getting dark she took Ginger back home with her and her children.

The next morning Mother Waggle said to her children and her foster-child, "Now, boys, first we are going to have a bath. We needn't go all the way to the brook today because I have a big bath of water ready behind the shed." Chattering noisily the little ducks went to the bath. Ginger followed reluctantly. Water.... he thought that word had a nasty sound and although he did not know what water really was, he was sure he would not like it at all. When they had come to the bath the little ducklings jumped into the water shouting with joy and splashed happily about. You could see that they were enjoying themselves but if a few drops of water fell on Ginger's fur, he shook them off crossly. Mother Waggle said that Ginger must be washed and that he must stand in the bath. Slowly he climbed on to the edge of the bath and very carefully dipped one paw into the water. Brr.... what a horrid feeling that was! So cold and so wet! He did not like it at all!

Ginger went bounding away. He had been right; he did not like water! Quacking loudly Mother Duck ran after him. She could not understand at all why the little pussy cat seemed to have such a dislike for water. When she found Ginger again he was up an apple tree and under the tree stood a young nannygoat, who was looking with surprise at the little acrobat. Anxiously Mrs. Waggle cried, "Come out of that tree at once, Ginger! It is far too dangerous. You might fall down, and that little goat won't do you any harm. You need not be afraid of her." "I am not afraid of that little goat," answered Ginger crossly. "I just wanted to have a good look at her, because I have never seen such an animal." He looked again at the little goat. "What an ugly animal," he thought, "I am glad that I don't look like that." Mrs. Waggle waited impatiently. "Come down at once, Ginger!" she said again, "Before you fall and hurt yourself!"

"It is not nearly so dangerous here in the tree as it is in the water," said Ginger, and stayed sitting calmly on the branch. The little ducks were having great fun. They found Ginger a good playmate. Mrs. Waggle shook her head. What had she let herself in for when she took this wild little cat under her wing? And the worst of it was that Ginger led her own children into all kinds of mischief. Just look, there sure enough were two of her children sitting beside Ginger on the branch! The little nanny-goat, who was angry at Ginger because he had made fun of her, had fetched her brother and he warned, "Just you make sure that you don't say any nasty things about my sister, or I'll teach you a lesson! When I grow bigger, I shall have horns and then I'll be able to hurt you!" This frightened Ginger a bit and he made sure that he kept safely out of reach of the little billy-goat. The mice, his friends, told the goat that Ginger had not meant to be nasty to his sister.

Each day little Ginger became wilder and more rough and at last Mrs. Waggle took her foster-child firmly in hand. Ginger was sorry and promised to improve and for the first few days he really behaved very well. He did not even climb up a tree but stayed playing quietly on the ground. It was quite impossible to get him into the water and at last Mother Waggle stopped trying. One day when Ginger was out for a walk with the Duck family they met the children of Mrs. Hen. Ginger thought they looked something like the Waggle family. They were just a little smaller. Still remembering what Mrs. Waggle had told him, he played for a long time very gently with the chickens and ducklings. Mother Waggle watched happily. Ginger really was a dear little animal, she thought. She just had to be firm with him sometimes. But then weren't all children sometimes naughty? Had she not been just the same herself when she was young? She smiled as she watched the children

playing peacefully. Day after day all went well with little Ginger. But one warm afternoon he began to get very tired of all the little chickens. They were so small and so busy and they were always running about and getting in his way. He had already spoken sharply to one or two of them and when once again he nearly fell over one of the chickens, he put his front paw smack on top of it. Oh dear, what a fright that little chicken got. The little ducks quacked with pleasure. They knew that Ginger would not really hurt the little chicken and they sometimes got a bit tired of the chicken family, just as Ginger did. Mrs. Waggle calmed Mrs. Hen who was very alarmed. The little chickens were really too small to play with someone like Ginger. He should have bigger playmates. Yes, Mrs. Waggle was very understanding. She wondered who would be a good friend for her little foster-child. Suddenly she knew. The rabbits!

Mother Waggle called Ginger and her own children and together they went to see the Rabbit family. The family did not seem to be at home and after looking for some time she found the three rabbit children sitting together under some large sunflowers. The three rabbits looked with surprise when they suddenly saw Ginger sitting up on his hind legs and heard him introduce himself so politely. They had never seen anything like this before. Mrs. Waggle was very pleased with her little foster-child. He knew now how to behave and she was glad that her training had not been in vain. The rabbits found Ginger a merry companion and Ginger got on very well with the three little rabbits. All four of them were about the same size and Ginger liked that very much. Every day they played together. But the little ducks felt sorry that Ginger had new friends and did not pay any attention to them now. They had always enjoyed their games together.

But it was not long before Ginger began to be naughty again. The warning words of Mrs. Waggle were soon forgotten and he thought more and more of mischief. They were continually encouraged in this by the young ducks, the mice and a little frog, who admired the four playmates very much. Whenever they could, they tried to do the same as the four friends but if they were too small to play one or other of the games they gathered round and cheered the rascals on. One day one of the rabbits wanted to gather berries. Of course he could have asked Ginger to climb in the bush and get the berries for him, but he thought it would be nicer to do it himself. "I will help you," promised Ginger, "I shall try to lift you up so that you can reach them." But although Ginger used all his strength he just could not manage to lift the rabbit up high enough to reach the berries and at last he gave up.

In the end Ginger was so naughty that he even began to tease Mrs. Waggle herself. To his great delight he found a ball of wool and for the fun of it, he tangled the wool all a-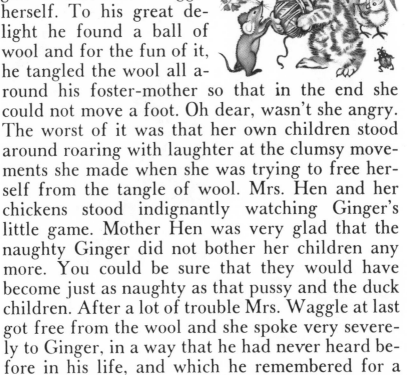round his foster-mother so that in the end she could not move a foot. Oh dear, wasn't she angry. The worst of it was that her own children stood around roaring with laughter at the clumsy movements she made when she was trying to free herself from the tangle of wool. Mrs. Hen and her chickens stood indignantly watching Ginger's little game. Mother Hen was very glad that the naughty Ginger did not bother her children any more. You could be sure that they would have become just as naughty as that pussy and the duck children. After a lot of trouble Mrs. Waggle at last got free from the wool and she spoke very severely to Ginger, in a way that he had never heard before in his life, and which he remembered for a long time afterwards.

Mrs. Waggle made up her mind that she would get her own back on Ginger for the trick he had played on her and it was not long before she saw her chance. In the orchard there stood a basket in which the farmer collected apples to take to the market. As she had expected, Ginger climbed one, two, three into the basket so that he could have a good look inside it, because Ginger liked to know everything. As soon as he was right inside, Mrs. Waggle lifted the lid up and let it fall shut with a snap. Poor Ginger was a prisoner inside. And wasn't he angry! He mewed loudly and from all directions the farm animals came running to see why Ginger was making such a terrible noise. They immediately felt sorry for their little friend and they used all their strength to lift up the lid of the basket. They tried several times and Mrs. Waggle was shaking with laughter when she saw the angry face of Ginger looking out from the basket.

But Ginger did not like

it at all. His whole life on the farm was not so happy now as it had been before and he longed to make a change. One evening not long after he had been shut in the basket, he crept quietly out of bed. Mother Waggle and her children were all sound asleep. Only the mice knew what he meant to do and they were already waiting outside for him with little lanterns to give him light. And what did Ginger do? He ran away! He did not want to be obedient any more to Mrs. Waggle. He wanted to be free to do exactly what he liked. Yes, that was very ungrateful of Ginger because Mrs. Waggle had looked after him so well during all that long time, just as if he had been one of her own children. But Ginger did not think of that.

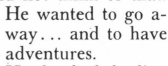

He wanted to go a-way... and to have adventures.
He thanked the little mice for their help and off he went .... I wonder where!